Embers of a Wayward Soul

Shreya Vijay

To my friends who think I'm an emotional Fort Knox - congratulations, this is your exclusive key. Don't lose it. I'm not making another copy.

I promise you, whatever you're looking for, it's all in here, somewhere.

PART 1

MISERY

listen, if you will, though I doubt it would make a difference, for there is none to be made, of course.

life is but a hollow vessel in which we are all condemned to toil - relentlessly since the dawn of our time until the twilight of it. often we are told it is a gift, yet it is nothing more than a cruel jest orchestrated by forces within our perception but beyond our understanding. years stretch on, each one indistinguishable from the last, each one a parade of suffering wrapped in the guise of meaning.

misery is our constant companion, the non-negotiable iron price we pay for our continued existence. the joke, however, lies in the reward, for it is no different.

misery for the price, misery for the prize.

a vicious cycle of torment, where meaning is promised but never delivered, where we stretch toward fulfilment only to find our hands clutching at dust and shadow of our past selves, each one slumped, bearing the cross of the existence of everything that we once were, everything that we couldn't be, and arguably, everything that we ultimately became.

you are born into it, life, without consent, and told to find purpose within it, a labyrinth built to deceive and confound. and so you wander, aimlessly but persistently, lost in this maze, the walls closing in until you're hit with the realisation of the futility of it all. you yearn for freedom, but what freedom can exist in a world where freedom itself is a burden? you look for gods, but find only their corpses, their promises as empty as the skies above.

but still, we endure. why? when even the creators have forsaken their most beautiful invention, when the orchestrator of the cosmos has turned its back on the despair of humanity—why do we, mere fleeting creatures adrift in the vast indifference of the universe, persist? what purpose does this unyielding struggle serve? what end awaits us in this senseless march toward oblivion?

we crawl forward, not out of hope, but out of some deep-rooted inertia, some primal instinct that compels us to live when life itself has lost its meaning. it is not for glory, nor salvation, nor even the false comfort of legacy. no, we persist without reason, without justification, as if defying the absurdity itself might somehow lend us the meaning we so desperately seek.

but it never does.

we endure because we cannot do otherwise—because, in this grand cosmic farce, even surrender has been stripped of its dignity.

and so, we remain — bound to this suffering, bound to this meaninglessness. misery, my dear, is both the key and the lock.

THE APOCALPYSE WAS QUIETER

the apocalypse was quieter than I thought.

no sirens, no chaos, no dramatic unravelling of the world I knew it. the world didn't roar or scream or burn. neither did it rumble beneath my feet or open up into a pool of lava. it didn't end with a fiery eruption or a cataclysmic crash. it was slow, like a breath that you know you're taking but doesn't quite reach your lungs.

the world ended with a whisper I couldn't hear, a shift I couldn't stop and a sinking ship I couldn't save. it just… faded. it ended in the quiet moments between my ragged heartbeats, in the moments when I realized that I was looking at the world falling apart at the seams but was no longer waiting for anything to change. one day, it was there, alive and chaotic, and then it wasn't.

the streets didn't scream. the sky didn't come falling down. instead, everything just slowed, like a clock winding down, until there was nothing but stillness. the silence settled in like dust while I stood there, waiting for the crash, the crescendo, the proof that something had happened, that I wasn't imagining it. but nothing came. pin. drop. silence. and it wasn't even peaceful. the silence around me was hollow like a vacuum begging to be filled with something - even if it was the remnants of my own soul.

the apocalypse was quieter because it wasn't outside - it was inside me. the wreckage, the ruin, the end of everything I believed in, it all happened here, behind my ribs, in the places I thought were unshakable. and what perplexed me the most was how quietly everything and everyone slipped away, as if I was the only one who hadn't figured it out yet.

yes, the world looks the same, but I don't. and that's the cruellest part: how the end of everything can feel so deafening in your chest yet leave the world around you entirely untouched.

THE ANATOMY OF APATHY

apathy isn't hollow -it's layered. It begins as exhaustion, a deep, bone-crushing fatigue that whispers, *Why bother?*

at first, it feels like a choice, a retreat from caring too much. the first time you notice it, it doesn't seem too deep - a missed call you don't return, a question you don't bother answering, another glass of alcohol when you knew you should've stopped at the last one, another cigarette dangling off the edge of your mouth even before you've finished your last one. and so, it spreads. the crack in your humanity becomes a fracture, and soon, you're caving in, folding in on yourself from the inside out. what starts as indifference hardens into something heavier, something you can't quite shrug off.

the mind becomes numb first, a fog settling in. your thoughts lag, then stop altogether, as if your brain decides it's safer to feel nothing than to risk the sting of disappointment again. you used to care, didn't you? well, fuck if you knew anymore. memories lose their edge. even the brightest moments seem dull, like photographs left too long in the sun. you just don't seem to *remember* anything.

next comes the heart. It doesn't shatter dramatically; it calcifies. the weight of feeling nothing presses down, squeezing out the last remnants of warmth. you hear a song, see a smile, and instead of stirring something, it just… bounces off. the heart doesn't ache anymore. it just exists, functional but distant, like a factory worker going through the same motions over and over and over and over… people talk to you, their voices buzzing like gnats, and you nod, you smile, you agree, but inside it's static. dead air.

you wonder if they can tell. you hope they can't. or maybe you hope they can. does it even matter? honestly? not really.

even your body betrays you. it drags itself forward, like a marionette with its strings tangled. you eat because it's what you're supposed to do and sometimes you just don't eat at all. you sleep because your eyes won't stay open, move because stopping feels just as meaningless. the mirror doesn't reflect you anymore, it shows a husk, a stranger, something half-finished and abandoned.

apathy is precise. it slices away at you with the care of a surgeon, removing pieces of you one by one. but there's no anesthesia, no sterile tools. it's messy and raw, and yet you just watch, unblinking, detached, as the scalpel cuts deeper and deeper. there's something almost fascinating about it, the way you disassemble yourself so willingly.

the cruellest part? you're still here. you're still *alive*. a pulse, a breath, a faint echo of something that used to be vibrant, and it's all wrong. it's all *wrong*. the rot is inside, hollowing you out, and all you can do is let it.

because fighting would mean you care. and caring would mean letting the hurt back in.

so, you just sit there, still and silent, waiting for the rest of you to disappear.

LONELINESS AT 2 AM

this is how loneliness feels at 2 am:

the clock ticks ritualistically like a slow, deliberate taunt, each second dragging me deeper into the kind of silence that feels alive, heavy, and watching. it's the predator and I'm its prey. it presses against my skin, seeping into my lungs until I'm choking on the back-breaking weight of nothing. I tried filling it with music, but even the songs sounded hollow, like they've grown tired of my company. so, I just don't try anymore - no music, no movies, no Netflix, no distractions; just me and this gaping void that I pretend I'm used to.

the wind outside howls like it knows something I don't, throwing itself against the window in a fury, wailing to be let inside. I almost want it to break the glass, to let the night swallow me whole, just so something feels real for a moment. the moon hangs there, all smug and distant, casting its cold light over this mess I call myself. it doesn't care that I haven't moved from my space in three whole days. why would it? why would anyone actually?

my breath catches every now and then, sharp and uneven, as if my body is protesting my refusal to cry. but tears are reserved for those whose hearts haven't frozen over, who can still feel something, anything, without it feeling like an insurmountable weight. plus, the tears feel useless, like throwing pennies into a well you know is dry. I press my hands against my chest, as if I can hold myself together in the palm of my hands, as if I can quiet the storm of memories clawing their way out and push them back in.

spoiler alert: so far, it doesn't seem to be working.

I tell myself I'm fine. I say it over and over, a mantra in the dark, but it sounds fake even to me. 'fine' feels like a lie. I'm not fine. I'm unspooling, thread by thread, into a version of myself I don't recognize, into a silence that doesn't just exist around me - it *is* me.

this is the sound of facing the truth: sometimes, I wonder if I'll ever feel like *me* again.

SAFE SPACE

I often think that there is no safe space for people like me.

if only I was what I once wanted to be.

when I was a kid, vivacious and full of energy

when my thoughts and actions were in a constant state of synergy.

but now, I'm trembling hands, creating chaos,

fighting my way against the whims of the cosmos.

I am a culmination of the missed chances I walked by,

I was too hung up on some things that I decided to not even try.

overtime, I became the overlooked pattern adorning the wallpaper,

granules of pepper filled in the explicitly labelled salt-shaker.

the quiet presence in the house, that seldom is felt,

writing crappy poetry in a corner, brimming with waves of regret.

my rage and anguish are domestic, I sharpen them every night,

in my own shadow, tucking them away until they're hidden from light.

I claim that my blood is darker than any wine ever brewed,

that my soul is tainted, and my heart is shrewd.

my lips spin a yarn – forging a fictitious narrative,

well, what can I say? I have always been supremely creative.

some days, it's easier to lie than to face the truth,

isn't that the biggest conundrum of the youth?

to spill the tea or hide the whole cup,

to try and be vulnerable or resort to armouring up?

so, I give it my all, I do my best,

I cope the way no one ever expects.

restraint and I, are strangers, always strung up on call,

anything that isn't everything feels like it's nothing at all.

my garden is overgrown with a multitude of weed, I overeat, I oversleep,

god, it's a vicious cycle of eat, sleep repeat!

I'm waiting for something better, letting go of something worse,

trying to find solace for my soul, trying to break this curse.

I've learnt not to let it mess with my head, you see?

maybe, there is just no safe space for people like me.

PART 2

YOU OUT OF ALL THE PEOPLE

you out of all the people were supposed to get it, you know?

you were the ones who were supposed to understand it all - the ones who could hear what I didn't say, the ones who could see through the walls I didn't even know I built. out of everyone in the entire goddamned fucking world, it was you. you were supposed to feel the cracks before they turned into fractures, to know when the smile was just a mask, when the laughter was hollow.

but lately, it feels like I'm standing in a room full of shadows, and none of them are you. it feels like I'm shouting into a void where only echoes answer, and none of them sound like you. you're still here, still laughing, still talking like nothing's changed. but everything has.

it's like we're living in parallel worlds that barely touch, like I'm watching you through glass that wasn't there before. you were supposed to know when I'm falling apart, to catch me before I even realized I was crumbling. but here I am, slowly coming undone, and you just keep living like everything's fine. I'm still part of the conversations, still showing up like nothing's wrong. yet inside, I'm screaming. I'm reaching out, and somehow, you don't see it, or maybe you do, but you've decided to turn away.

I'm not even sure you see me anymore. I'm right here, but I'm invisible. and it breaks my heart in ways I didn't think possible because it wasn't supposed to be like this. it's like I'm drowning in plain sight, and you don't notice - or worse, you notice, and you do nothing, because I always got it, right? I keep waiting for you to ask, to check in, to pull me aside like you used to, just to make sure. but instead, I get empty conversations about nothing.

it's hard to keep pretending like everything's fine when inside, I'm wondering if you even care enough to ask. and the thing is, I never thought I'd have to ask you to care. I never thought I'd have to beg for your attention, for your understanding, for you to see me the way you always used to - without me having to perform my pain, to put it on display.

you know, I always thought friendship meant showing up for each other, no matter what. And I did that - I always showed up for you. even when I was breaking inside, when everything in me screamed to stay in bed, to disappear for a while, I still showed up. I put my pain in a box, locked it up, and pretended it didn't exist because that's what friends do, right? we push our own storms aside to stand in the rain with each other.

there were nights when I stared at the ceiling, wondering if it was worth it to wake up in the morning, but I still reverted to each text, answered each call, still showed up the next day. and now, it feels like you wouldn't even notice if I didn't. you wouldn't even ask if I was okay because you're too used to me being the strong one, the one who never needs anything back.

when I was drowning in my own darkness, when it felt like every breath was a battle I didn't want to fight, why didn't you answer when I was knocking? when I felt like dying, when I could barely scrape myself together, I was there, holding space for everyone around me, while my own world was burning down. I was there when I had nothing left to give, and I gave anyway. and you know the worst part? you didn't even notice. or maybe you did, but you thought it wasn't your problem. thought I could handle it on my own, just like I always do.

I showed up for everyone when I didn't even want to show up for myself. I buried my own grief, my own pain, because someone needed me. but now I wonder, why do I always have to be the level-headed one? do I not have the right to break down once in a while and actually be able to lean on someone other than myself? when will it be my turn to fall apart, to ask for help, and not feel like I'm asking for too much?

I really don't wanna be that alone. but I guess I am.

I felt like I was dying, and you didn't even know. oh, and what's worse is that I shouldn't have had to scream for you to hear it in the first place.

I don't know how to explain it any clearer than this, but then again, I never thought I'd have to explain it to you at all.

NOTHING

I expect people to know how to care for me, to read between the lines I've never even uttered. I expect them to know me - know *Shreya* - when I've never trusted them enough to give them a single clue.

I've never felt safe enough to let them in, to let them walk through the wreckage of my mind, flirt with the sharp edges of my sanity, or find the places I need to be held. all I've done is push them away, pretending I'm fine, pretending I'm whole, and then sit in the empty quiet, shattered by the weight of their absence - as if they ever had a chance to unearth the buried fragments of myself I spent years hiding.

how could they know?

how could they give me what I've spent my whole life denying I even wanted? and still, it breaks me when they believe the lie and give me exactly what I asked for – Nothing.

SILENCE

I immediately go silent when something upsets or hurts me.

not out of strength, not out of resilience. it's just a reflex, like touching fire and pulling away. words feel too heavy, too sharp, so I swallow them whole, letting them sit like stones in my chest, bearing down until there isn't enough space for me to breathe, let alone say the words.

it's easier this way, to fold inward and disappear behind the wall I've built brick by brick.

everyone finds it absurd, but I retreat because the alternative is unbearable. to stay and feel it all, to let it crack me open, would mean exposing the parts of me I've tried so hard to bury.

and what if I say it all and still make no difference? so, my silence is a shield, and I wear it like armour, even when it suffocates.

the world keeps spinning, oblivious, and I shrink further, smaller and smaller, until I'm not sure there's anything left of me to find. it's not strength. it's survival. but in the quiet, the hurt doesn't fade - it festers, a constant ache that I pretend doesn't exist.

I tell myself this is control, that I'm choosing this numbness. the truth? it's fear. I'm just scared. scared of what will happen if I let the silence break.

WHICH VERSION OF MYSELF DID I KILL?

"Which version of yourself did you kill to become this calm?"

I killed the version that yearned to be seen,

the version that wouldn't hesitate to kick, cry or scream.

I gutted the one that craved care and attention,

the one that walked through fire just to get an iota of cold affection.

I subdued the one who was nothing but a soft-hearted crier,

the one who'd sell her soul just to taste the shadow of indifferent desire.

I refused to any longer yield to the one that made me feel,

all sorts of emotions that, every night, brought me to my fucking knees.

I beheaded the one that told me I wasn't enough,

the one who was never audacious to call anyone out on their bluff.

I killed the one who wore her heart on her sleeve,

who would give and give—only to be left bereaved.

I crucified the one who reached out, hands trembling, pleading,

I pulled her back, let her drown, and left her bleeding.

I ripped apart the one who always conceded,

for if she could not be loved, she had to be needed!

"If I am of no use to them, how do I justify my presence in their lives?

how do I keep myself from vanishing right before their eyes?"

shush, my sweetheart, shut the fuck up; and give in to your demise.

It wasn't planned - no, it wasn't kind or clean.

it didn't make me feel reborn, just hollowed out, stripped to the bone,
a calmness that feels more like a tomb than a throne.
pitch black, flesh and blood,
a quiet violence buried beneath the flood.
the rage has built a home in my chest,
it feels like it won't ever digress, won't ever rest!

but calmness demands a steep price,
a silence forged by the armours of shrouds in the battlefield, left behind
after all, this calm is a graveyard, a hollowed-out skin,
the silence left after a war waged within.

BURNING BRIDGES

I burn bridges just to watch the ashes fall.

all my relationships, my friends, my bonds, my lifelines are getting fed into a shredder, piece by piece, and I just can't bring myself to care. the faces I once knew like the back of my hand now blur into one indistinct mass, their voices lost in the static. I don't even try to make sense of what they say as they all take a leap off the ledge - cut off their losses.

the fire in my eyes starts small, a spark in the corner of my mind, and I watch it grow, swallowing everything I once called important. the flames lick at the edges of everything, devouring the fragments of who I was, who I thought I could be.

I don't flinch.

I don't blink.

it's as if the heat doesn't even touch me anymore. it's just another thing; another part of the wreckage I call life.

smoke fills the air, thick and violent but I breathe it in deep, like I'm inhaling my own destruction.

and why shouldn't I? I earned it, after all.

there's no coughing, no choking - just calm, clinical detachment. they burn. they scream.

honestly, maybe something inside of me does too.

but I don't listen. I'm too busy feeding the fire with the final remnants of my sanity, my capricious emotions and my ability to care.

and when the last of it dies out, when I have wrung myself dry of every last bit of humanity left in me and the ruins are just ashes under my feet, I won't feel anything.

when the charred remains of my past are nothing more than dust, will I mourn? will I feel anything? relief? loss?

no, just the cold, empty power of knowing I've erased it all—and nothing fucking matters anymore.

and then? then, I'll smile, because in the end, it's all just a game.

I won.

WHEN THE UNIVERSE REFUSES TO CONSPIRE

when the universe turns its back on you, it feels like yearning for someone that doesn't even know you exist.

it's like waiting at a door that never opens, even though you've knocked until your hands are raw. you keep hoping for a flicker - a sound, a sign, a shadow moving behind the cracks but there's nothing. just silence. heavy, unkind silence.

I look to the skies, my chest full of prayers I don't even believe in anymore, hoping that something, anything, will answer back. but the stars stay still, frozen in their apathy, and the wind passes right through me as if I'm nothing but a phantom - an invisible creature undeserving of being on Earth.

it feels like being abandoned by something you never truly had, like chasing the echo of a voice that was never meant for you. you keep running, keep calling out, but there's no one there, no one ever was. it's the realization that you've been clinging to shadows, pouring your heart into a game where the players left long ago, leaving you to move pieces on a board that no longer matters.

it's not just loneliness. it's the bitter taste of having believed so deeply in something that was never real, of watching your hopes collapse into nothing but dust and the faint memory of what you thought it could be. you're left standing in the middle of it all, hands empty, heart heavy, wondering if you ever even belonged in the first place.

the waiting doesn't just stretch, it hollows. every second aches, carving out pieces of me I didn't know could hurt.

and then it hits, sharp and final: the universe doesn't care. it never cared. it lets you sit there, stripped bare, waiting for miracles that don't exist, until all you can do is stand up and walk away. not because you've found peace, but because there's nothing left to wait for.

IT WASN'T SUPPOSED TO FEEL THIS WAY

it wasn't supposed to feel this way, you know?

it wasn't supposed to feel like a knife is wedged between my ribs and every time my heart beats, it can feel the prick of that knife slice through the surface, deeper and deeper with each successive thud. it was supposed to be freeing; I was supposed to be happy after it all. really happy. but where has this gotten me?

I wasn't supposed to spend hours looking in the mirror trying to perfect the ridges of my smile, I wasn't supposed to work so much that I don't even have time to breathe, I wasn't supposed to start wearing full sleeves in the middle of the summer and I wasn't supposed to start zoning out in the middle of conversations. again. all this wasn't supposed to happen again. this makes me sound quite ungrateful, doesn't it?

lately I've been residing in the quiet corner of my heart where gratitude and longing intertwine. every day is a delicate dance between the appreciation of what I have and the bittersweet ache of what could've been. for every cherished moment I hold close, there lingers a whisper of the roads I didn't, the roads I couldn't take, and the dreams that I left behind. it's after 20 years of my life that I realized it's possible to love what you have and still grieve for what could've been. but I always have the option of just not thinking about it, right?

well, the things I refuse to think about are so adamant that they have forced their way into my dreams. I am so tired of opening my eyes in the morning and wishing that I had never closed them in the first place. the horrors that never happened are imprinted in the back of my eyelids. I wake up every night gasping for a breath that was never taken from me. my mind keeps reeling out the same imprint of a splatter of blood that I have never seen – not yet at least.

there's a little girl in my head and she keeps screaming "unloved! unworthy! undeserving!" at every moment in my life; so much so that I have started to believe her. I never knew I felt so much and so hard until I had to sit down with my thoughts, trying to structure them into a string of a combination of 26 letters.

I know everything that hurts so bad always starts with a subtle ache but this… I wasn't supposed to feel like this.

I wasn't supposed to feel anger that burns me from the inside. it resides in the cave at the bottom of my stomach, simmering and boiling until it has reached my organs, shrivelling them until every atom in my body that makes me, me, is burned beyond recognition. it reached my lungs, filling them with smoke, overflowing as it makes its way up my throat.

I wasn't supposed to feel exhaustion that infests a single cell but multiples until it has ravaged half of my body, still growing until it has devoured everything it can reach. the kind of exhaustion that flows through my bloodstream, covering it in the ashes of my burned organs, coating it black.

I wasn't supposed to feel this crippling fear that leaves me shaken and forlorn every time I let it rise to the surface. it's never forgotten, always festering between the knuckles of my clenched fists, dripping from the tips of my fingers. I don't know what I am more afraid of, my feelings or who I would be without them.

I have a lot of bad habits. I bite my nails, I scratch at my skin, I am incoherent with my words, chaos reigns my thoughts, I intentionally eat food that I am allergic to, I dye my hair until they are practically falling out and I hardly ever tell people that I am not doing well. I lie unnecessarily and often. and yet, I think one of my worst habits is not voicing my discomfort when it actually matters.

I would raise hell if my clothes weren't to my liking, but I would never tell anyone to give me space even when I desperately need it. I will whine relentlessly about not getting a grade that I desperately wanted, but I won't let a flicker of fatigue mar my expressions. I will kick and scream about wanting to visit some random place but won't ever explicitly vocalize my discomfort at having to settle and compromise.

instead, I will grin and bear it. I will say the right words, imitate the right actions, feign the perfect amount of excitement, empathy, pain, or sadness that is expected of me, but I would never be honest and tell them, tell anyone, to stop. I won't tell them to stop and let me breathe, to let me feel what I am feeling because if I (or rather they) can't logically explain my behaviour, my feelings, they aren't valid. and yet, in the blanket of the night, when I stand in the front of my mirror, staring at the reflection of a person who is me, but also isn't me, with the accusatory glint in her eyes, I can't help but feel the unfiltered surge of emotions hit me like a wave.

you know why I don't prefer to talk about things? because if I talk about it, that means it matters and if it matters, it is real, and if it's real, it's going to hurt. it's going to *fucking hurt*. but if I keep it inside of me, I can always go on pretending that it's all in my head. if I don't let go of that tight leash I have around my emotions, I keep up the appearances.

after all, I've been horrible at letting things go, until I do. and then, I let go hard enough to send everything around me crumbling into the dust; the bricks and mortar of the home that I built shattered into a gazillion particles of cement and tar; the veins in my hand bursting until crimson pools out staining the white marbles beneath my feet. just like my nightmares.

I'm dramatic, I know. it's times like these, I wish I was more like my family. I wish I was more like my mother who wears her heart on her sleeves. I wish I was more like my father – analytical and smart. I wish I was more like my younger brother, able to compartmentalize and differentiate. I wish I was more like my elder brother, unapologetically enforcing uninfringeable boundaries or like my best friend, who knows how to ask for help when she needs it.

anything would be better than who and what I am right now.

but when I stared at myself in the mirror today, just for a fleeting moment, I froze. one single second and after days or keeping it together, I snapped. I dropped. my knees collided with the ground.

and I screamed.

it tore out of my throat, as my clenched fists pressed harshly against my stomach. my head was bowed, and I wailed, and shrieked, and yelled until my voice was raw and then I screamed some more.

nobody came to comfort me. my fists began pounding against the cold hard floor, ripping open my skin, bruising my bones with no blood coming from the wound and once I am done breaking apart, there was no mark left on my unblemished skin.

PART 3

WHO DO YOU RUN TO?

Who do you run to when nothing in the world seems to play out right?

When the deserted corridor of your mind twists and turns,
Into an endless labyrinth where hope crashes and burns.
Where every single door opens into a new realm of chaos and confusion,
Where the constant voices in your head are more than just an illusion
Where the demons you once hid, hunt in the wild; no longer just a dream
In moments you're both the hunter & hunted, the whisper and the scream.
So, who do you run to?

When the shadows stretch long, eating away at the light,
Your nightmares stepping into the arena, forgoing the confines of the night.
When the comfort of the silence turns into a deafening roar,
And every beat of your heart reminds you of the dread you can't ignore.
Every breath you inhale amounts to an insurmountable struggle,
When your will to live and thrive is buried deep underneath the rubble.
Who do you run to?

When the walls around you close in, dark and tight,
And the echo of your own footsteps haunts you in the middle of the night.
When you run, run and run through the endless maze,

The sinister silence makes you crave a scream to shatter the haze.

Where silence is the currency of barter,

And your very soul is being sacrificed at the sacred altar.

Who do you run to?

When you find yourself in a room of mirrors, reflecting fractured lies,

Every image in sight, more distorted, each one a disguise.

When the glass - cold to the touch - mocks your every move,

And your twisted reflection betrays an unbearable truth.

When you feel the aching pain that just won't subside,

And face the ghosts of your past that never truly died.

Who do you run to?

When you hate what you see in the mirror?

And your hands, a glove of blood, the telltale signs of an inveterate sinner.

When the faces staring back aren't your own, but a haunted parade,

Your ancestors, your descendants, all sharing the same grim masquerade.

When you finally realise, you're caught in a trap with no way out,

And you kick and scream, you beg and shout.

Who do you run to?

When a soft mournful tone, breaks through the haze,

And you finally realise you haven't slept well in days.

When you finally bear witness to a harbinger of dread,

You venture deeper into your conscience where shadows fearlessly tread.

When you walk through the corridors, with your heart in your hand,

And every fleeting moment passes through time like shifting quicksand.

Who do you run to?

When you notice the memories painted on walls, each one a trap,

And you find yourself in a haunting gallery where the distant past overlaps.

When the faces in the portraits watch with hollow, piercing eyes,

And their silent judgement punctuates your muted cries.

When you try to look away, but their gaze pulls you back,

And you get sucked into the depths of your darkest black.

Who do you run to?

When you scream so loud that the mirrors along with your sanity shatter,

And each tile of the walls is covered in insidious blood splatters.

When the relentless world outside doesn't wait,

And the shadows step into you, sealing your fate.

When you fall to your knees, the weight crushing your will,

And you're screaming into the void, time standing still.

Who do you run to?

When the void remains silent, your plea a lost song,

And then a whisper emerges, eerily strong.

When unwanted hands caress your skin,

Worshipping your torment like a sacrificial hymn.

When you recognize your own voice, twisted by despair,

And you feel tempted to give in to the darkness that ensnares.

Who do you run to?

When the whisper grows louder, a haunting refrain,

And a symphony of sorrow melts into a chorus of pain.

When the walls finally close in, the light fades away,

And sanity crumbles to dust, your very essence feels betrayed.

When the portraits bleed, their eyes now blind,

And you're pulled into an abyss, leaving reason behind.

Who do you run to?

When in that final moment, the last beam of light leaves your weary eyes,

And you can feel a piece of you has shrivelled up and died.

When the darkness isn't just around, it's a part of you,

And there's a scar on your soul, a mark of the ruse.

When the last remnants of sanity slip through your trembling grasp,

And the whispers of madness are all that you have left to clasp.

Who do you run to?

When your world collapses into a sombre, spectral haze,

And the icy grip ensnares you in an unyielding maze.

When you stand alone where shadows waltz and nightmares breed,

You're trapped in the depths of darkness, with no light to lead.

When everything you've ever known unravels in a symphony of despair,

And the very fabric of reality is stripped fucking bare,

It begs the question:

When there's no one to run to, no saviour in sight.

Who do you run to when nothing in the world seems to play out right?

THE SHADOW THEY SHAPED

I often myself wondering whether it's okay to miss someone who is the reason behind my sleepless nights – especially when once it was the sound of their heartbeats that lulled me to sleep? whether it is okay to yearn for the arms that choked me, especially when they once held me steady and strong.

it's hard for me to acknowledge that today fear melts on my tongue every time your name pops up in a conversation. it's difficult for me to admit that you terrify me, my love. for so long I've been standing in front of this mirror, staring at my reflection, but seeing yours. it's a relentless struggle – looking into my dark brown eyes and seeing your face, as well as I remember it, being reflected in those pools. the bracelets on my hand and the slangs infused in my language are a constant reminder that at the place where I am standing right now, you once existed.

it makes me hate myself, you know?

it makes me hate the way I look, the way I dress, the way I speak; but above all, it makes me hate the way I look. so forlorn and desolate that even an apathetic person would trip over themselves, weeping alongside my reflection. but, if I hate all that you've built including my own damn self, I should hate you too, right? well, however painful it is to admit, everything that I once loved has transitioned into something I fear.

the numbness has been spreading in my cells like an amoeba reproducing. every bit of laughter has been replaced with bouts of sadness and yet, I am suffering from alexithymia. it's all been so difficult that the only survival tactic I could come across was forgetting. all of it. your voice, your hugs, your jokes that made my ears bleed, and everything else that reminds me of you. but, then again, how can a person survive after forgetting themselves?

so, maybe, I should let it all go. maybe if I opened up, it would hurt less, right? I still remember the times when you used to say my name with such softness. if your voice, when speaking my name was a font, it would resemble elegant cursive. but now, the strokes of that cursive font have sharpened into the edges of a typewriter font – sharp, mundane and harsh.

you once used to say my name with reverence, like it was something you were holding with everything inside of you. today, you spit it out like a curse drawn from Tartarus – the deepest, darkest and evilest pits of the underworld. then, I had to place a hand on my chest to keep my heart from flying out and landing onto your palms but today, I am down on my knees, trying to bubble wrap the pieces of my shattered heart.

the imaginary battle vines that I had been fighting in my head since the moment you stepped into my life have now become roots. a warzone of rashes has broken out like plague underneath my cracked skin, shrouding it with angry red – red that symbolizes your anger and resentment and cracks that symbolize my misery.

if I speak out all these words that have been weighing down on my chest, I would finally be able to breathe, wouldn't I? but it all boils down to whether anyone would believe me. just this mere thought is enough to drench me in apprehension, to make the fear billow in my lungs because if I am being honest with myself, I would admit that nobody would believe a word I am saying.

after all, who would ever believe a victim without a scratch?

another tactic down the drain. as I keep staring into the mirror, heaviness weighing down my body, I am hit with an epiphany – not one that gives me respite though, not by a long shot. but maybe that is the only way I will be able to survive this. What do you do when no matter how hard you try, you just can't seem to escape the heaviness? you feel.

you feel every part of your sorrow and anguish until the noose around your neck loosens. you pay attention to your feelings and thoughts, your doubts and insecurities so that they're no longer a stranger to you. you have a name for them. and someone once told me that a name is a very powerful thing.

so, I'll stand here, and I'll feel it. I will look into my reflection and analyse every nook and cranny of my reflection to find something that is uniquely mine. something can become my Achilles Heel – something that will keep me grounded while I fling my body into the River Styx, hoping to become invulnerable.

there, under those dark waters that symbolize loathing of death, I will make friends with the darkness simmering beneath the surface of my skin until we are one, until we are meshed together, eternally inseparable. and when we move, we will move as two shadows – one bigger and one smaller.

shush now, don't fear me, my love. after all, you are the one who made me turn into a monster.

14

TO THE ONES I COULDN'T LOVE ENOUGH

to the ones I couldn't love enough –

it has been twenty-one years today, and I still have that photograph tucked in one of the boxes up in the attic. the one we clicked when we were still young and thought that the world revolves around us. eyes crinkling, mouths spread in a face- splitting grin that seemed to stretch as far as the Amazon, our hands around each other's waists, we stood on the beach. I can still feel the waves hitting our legs, the scarf I had around my neck whipping through the wind like a cape. I look at it and I am reminded of the happy days and how scared it made me feel that I am opening up to a bunch of people who I've just met.

so, I pushed you all away.

I hated myself so loudly that I didn't even hear your love. and that's on me. so, when this feeling of incessant grief strikes me, I let myself drown in it because I deserve it.

grief – as I so recently realized is just love that has no place to go. you have so much love to give but no one to give it too. yet, everything that is in the world has to manifest itself one way or the other.

so, this love finds its way into the lump in your throat, it crystalizes into tears in the corner of your eyes and weighs down your heart, molding itself into the hollow feeling in your chest. everything that once was, is not anymore and it hurts. it *pains* that the things and people you once took for granted are nowhere near you now.

I hold too much of this grief inside of me and sure, sometimes, it gets too heavy to bear. but when I transfer the burden from my shoulders to my hands, ready to unload it, I often find myself wondering where can I even put it down. so, until the time I can put it on my shoulders again, I leave small traces of this baggage I carry on the things and persons I touch. I bleed on people that didn't cut me, smash the dreams that once gave me the air to breathe and push away the only people who ever seemed to care about me. I stain them with agony and regret, and then I have the audacity to question why I ruin everything that I ever touch.

my love for you guys was like the last days of someone's life – disheartening and never enough, always waiting for the other shoe to drop. yours, on the other hand, was like counting the stars – unrequited, endless and perpetual in the vast sky.

I know we made more than just a few copies of this photograph and honestly, I am not sure if you deemed it best to preserve our love like this. in fact, I wouldn't blame you if you decided to set these tattered photos on fire. you can burn down every single one of our memories because you loved me too much and now looking at these photos and revisiting those memories instigate a heartburn.

honestly, and I know you probably won't ever believe me, but I remember the days when silence spoke for us, when our emotions and feelings were too much to remain in the same room. I remember the days we would reminisce, and you'd beg me to let you in but my walls had come up so high and so fast, there was nothing any of us could've done to change that. finally, I remember the days when I watch you walk out of my house and never return – one by one but in a haunting synchrony.

one of the biggest regrets, the biggest source of grief we humans accumulate in ourselves is of not knowing when it was the last time for something. I hope that in the future, they invent this small golden light which shines bright whenever something is about to end. so that when it was the last time I'd see you, I would know and realization would've slapped me in the face before it was too late.

if I could go back in time and do it all over again, I know I'd do things differently. because if this is the aura of the ending, I want to rewrite this story – I want to rewrite our story. but…

well, at least for this lifetime, we will keep this love in this tattered photograph where everything was perfect – even if it was just for a heartbeat.

15

I FORGOT TO TEXT BACK

I'm sorry I forgot to text you back.

for what it's worth, I wasn't busy. I wasn't caught up in work or out living some great adventure. I just... didn't.

I stared at your message, felt the pull to respond, and then let it sit there like it didn't matter. like *you* didn't matter.

and the worst part? it wasn't because I didn't care. it's because I didn't know how to care in a way that felt right. I didn't know how to pick up my phone, type something real, and send it without feeling like I was giving away too much or saying too little.

so instead, I chose nothing.

I let the silence speak for me, hoping it wouldn't scream what I was too much of a coward to say.

I tell myself it's fine, that you'll understand, that the silence doesn't sting as much as it probably does. but deep down, I know that's a lie.

and honestly, love? a part of me likes it - the way the guilt crawls under my skin, the way the silence builds a wall I can hide behind. it's twisted, I know, but maybe this is what I deserve. to push people away just far enough that they stop waiting, so I can finally be alone with the mess I've made of myself.

after all, maybe that's all I've ever been good at.

16

A WOUND THAT NEVER HEALS

what are we even trying to save when there is nothing left?

lately, I've been thinking a lot about all the bones that I let other people break so that they could cradle me close to their bodies. it gave me a sense of reassurance and dare I say it – love. I let them whip me left and right, enduring all the verbal lashes, and I smiled. yes, darling, I fucking smiled. because since the moment I met them, in the middle of enemy territory, when nothing seemed to be going my way, I was more theirs than I was mine.

I am a curious mutation being modified every single second of every single minute. I have my mom's smile – it is evident in the way the right side of my lips curls more than the left. I inherited my dad's inquisitiveness which peeks through every time I demand to know the 'why' behind any statement. I have accumulated my younger sibling's stubbornness and my elder sibling's relentlessness which are fighting at the forefront helping me navigate this maze called life. I have incorporated my ex best friend's mannerisms and way of speaking; and my colleague's mindset has somehow influenced my own – every single place and every single person I've ever met has had an influence on my life.

This body, as I said before, has never ever been my own.

I think that is why I abhor the idea of leaving so much because when someone does leave, you have to learn how to forget the way they breathe. to save yourself from further heartbreak, you never to unlearn everything that you leant in their presence and in doing so, you erase a part of yourself from existence – a part that once flourished is now nothing more than a painful reminder of the past. And something like this, is bound to be catastrophic.

As a defence mechanism, I wrote poems to stop the bleeding in my chest from coming out as cough residue every time I opened my mouth to address them. the blood in my chest was enough to drown my lungs which made breathing ten times worse – but I endured it all. the strokes of my ink pen are where I exist when I can't stomach everything I have been served. My proses are the hand I place on my throat to keep myself from getting sick and laying myself bare instinctively.

honestly, I haven't been myself lately, except, I've been exactly like myself. I broke my ribs in two so that I could tuck both the parts within themselves, curl them up and shiver in their hold – feeding in the warmth that I hoped I would get from you. I want to crawl into myself, fold myself into a million little pieces until I'm small enough to occupy the spaces between the atoms that make up our world.

you asked me how I am even alive because humans die before they turn this cold. I didn't even flinch, so I think maybe you were right. I am not human after all. just a hollow skeleton littered in scars.

but do you know what it feels like to have a wound that never heals? I, for one, know that you don't. because every time you scratched yourself, there was someone to patch you back up. I am slightly ashamed to mention that I was one of those 'someone' too. once upon a time.

you know how when you visit a hospital to get a bodily wound treated, they disinfect it with ethanol, which, by the way, is just a fancy word for alcohol. but the wounds you left behind are significantly obscured and resistant to the traditional medical treatments.

the gashes you sculpted with enormous patience and artistic prowess have taken the form of craters lining the walls of my veins and the moulded themselves into dentures that fit all my internal organs. all this time, I have fed them the embers of my hope and aspirations, dreams and desires, until they were nothing but a collection of embers burning bright in the cracks and crevices of my body, sometimes seeping through the pores.

so, I don't think it's even remotely surprising that I need vodka infused in my bloodstream, coursing through my veins because that is the only way I can ever heal. but then again what if I don't want to heal?

because that is the scariest part of getting better. you have to tell people about all the times you've had it worse, and I don't think I am strong enough to do that just yet. so, until I am strong enough to let it all out in the open, I'll be right here, lamenting what we had, what we were and how in a blink of an eye, it all went down in flames. just like the liquor running through my veins leaving more burns that ever before.

and that, mi amor, is what it feels to have a wound that never heals.

17

LOVER OF MINE

dear lover,

my stomach is full of the confessions I refused to give words to while yours are eating dust at the edge of my car's dashboard – where you left them the last time we met. I think it's because we are too afraid to be lonely that we keep holding on tighter than ever before. we fear the free fall, so we keep holding on to the pointy fence regardless of how much it hurts.

it's second nature to want to cling on to the sense of familiarity, even if it is the sting of poison. after all, that is what we're taught, right? if you ingest the poison for long enough, you'll be immune to its effects. you'd learn to crave it even. and I think that is *exactly* what I did with you.

I write about people who are significant to me. writing about them makes it easier for me to make sense of all my disorganized thoughts and feelings that have me putting myself through a blender. so, I wrote about you too. but I've never been the one to think of the consequences, as you very well know. because today, when I flip through these pages, you're here again. in every sentence, and time and again, these sentences make me think of you, vividly. so, I had this another thought, which, as you can see, has been transformed into another write-up.

years from today, when I pick it up, I'll again be reminded of you and we can't have that now, can we? having your face in my mind is so troublesome, that I carved the edges of the strokes of my pen to represent every dent in your face. if words could form a picture, this letter, my love, would be your face.

I think you'll be happy knowing that while these words are flowing from my fingertips, my ears are filled with the melodies of your favorite band – the one you used to put on repeat, every time we went driving. if nothing else, this is making me feel the sting of our parting even more bitterly because amplifying my discomfort would serve well for this letter.

all my friends keep asking me why I don't look happy anymore, why I don't smile. between you and me, it's because I've always associated the feeling of happiness with you. the hurt, the pain, it all came way after. so, every time even a sliver of happiness shines on me, I'm transported back to our times together and I spiral. just this time, I have no one to turn to.

thinking about you always leaves bitterness in its wake. sure, it's in the aftertaste but it's bitterness regardless. so, I force myself to think of the bad and the humiliating, the sad and the enraging because I can't go back to what and how we were. sure, our song might be built on the tunes of happy music but at the end of the day, it is riddled with sad lyrics – lyrics that punch me in the chest and rile me up every time I try to skim through them. and sometimes, the hardest part is knowing when to let go.

someone once told me that it is possible for two truths to co-exist. I never believed them. but today, as we stand side by side, it all falls into perspective. you can love me and still not want me. I can hate you, but your presence can still make me feel better. we can be so bad for one another and yet, make the perfect team. we can heal each other's wounds but still leave gashes in our wake. and you did, leave gashes, I mean. I think I'll remember this forever, it won't ever wane. it'll follow me around for the rest of my life, shadowing me and making its presence known. or maybe not.

trust me, love, I want to forget what it feels like to write about you. but you're the cure to my writer's block. my pen will refuse to write anything about anyone but when it comes to you, it never says no. all my ideas stem from you, all the agony I've channelled in my write-ups is curtesy of you; but I don't want it anymore.

I've always been the one living in the moment, you see. but today, I'm thinking of my future. I am thinking of what and how my future self would feel if she ever read this letter and it has me trembling in fright. because if she does end up reading this, she'll need someone to lean on and out of all the lessons you've ever taught me, this one did stick – you're on your own and you'll always be on your own. everything you know and love and was once accustomed to will be gone. everything but one – grief.

so, to spare her any torment, I'm sending this letter to you. somewhere I won't find it ever again. maybe you won't even read it, or maybe you would, and you just won't care – like you never did – and tear this into little pieces before it fucks up your sanity.

but whatever be the fate of this letter, it will never, ever, find its way into the hands of future me. she will not be subjected this this kind of insanity.

nevertheless, before saying the final goodbye, you remember our philosophical discussions? well, wasn't it my chance to shoot a question? after months of thinking and contemplating, I got one for you –

out of all the things and all the people to abandon me, why couldn't it have been grief?

with love,
someone you probably don't even think about

PART 4

18.

LOVING YOU WAS AN ACT OF SELF-HARM

loving you was like holding onto a rope that was slowly unravelling, convinced that if I just gripped it tighter, it would hold.

at first, it felt strong, secure, like the knot was something I could trust. but over time, I felt it slip through my fingers, strand by strand, until I was left grasping at threads that weren't even real anymore. every pull I made only seemed to loosen it further, but I kept holding on, thinking it was the only thing keeping me from falling.

I kept pretending that the tug in my chest wasn't tearing me apart, that the weight of it wasn't pulling me down further. every time I gave, you took, and every time I needed you, you were just out of reach. but I convinced myself that love meant being okay with the slow fraying, that this is what it was supposed to feel like.

So, I kept holding, kept hoping the rope would somehow mend itself, that my grip could somehow make everything whole again.

but in the end, I realized I wasn't just holding onto the rope - I was becoming it.

each thread that slipped through my fingers was a piece of me I couldn't get back. I didn't notice how much I was losing until I was nothing but frayed edges, a fragile thing that barely resembled the person I once was. loving you didn't fill me up; it hollowed me out, until the space between us was all I could feel.

now, I'm left with the echo of that rope, and the bitter truth that sometimes, holding on is what destroys you.

19

I DON'T KNOW HOW TO LOVE IN MODERATION

I don't know how to love in moderation. I either love too much or not at all. this is now a pattern – something that I only recently noticed. I either dive headfirst into the deep end or I feel like there is some intangible cosmic force that keeps me from even dipping my toes into the water.

I either fall in love heart-first, head second or run to the ends of the earth the moment it starts feeling right. either way, whatever path I choose, leaves me gasping for breath, writhing in pain in the agony of love or despair, unbearable warmth or excruciating cold that I can feel in the crease of my arms, the curl of my lips, or the space between my eyebrows. every emotion leaves me feeling like I am standing in the eye of the storm or at the center of an eclipse. I am either gambling everything that I am as everything around me turns to dust or I am standing in the juncture of something miraculous yet explosive.

whatever I say leaves me feeling as if I've taken a mouthful of a scalding hot drink that is gradually liquefying my insides as love, so much love pours out of my atoms, crystalizing at my skin. after all, my friends always said that I had too much love to give. and yet –

I can't tell my mom that I love her until I have literal tears pooling at the edge of my eyes, until my love for her that occupies every single cell inside

my body is screaming, begging to be released- it's only then that I tell her
– "mom, I love you. I love you. I love you."

I can't my friends that I love them until I am drunk enough to forego my limitations. my siblings? I can't tell them at all.

I know I don't have to. they know it already. but sometimes, I am so overwhelmed by this feeling inside of me that I feel if I don't put it into words, I will explode. the words will push their way out of my chest like a baby forcing its way out of its mother's womb and leave me coated in blood. sometimes I hear them laugh, I see them suppressing a grin by pressing their lips together, cracking a lame joke that would make a rock stare at them in amusement, hold my hand as a way to reassure me that 'it's okay, I'm here for you. I got you.' or just exist in the same space as me – without saying a word, just us sipping our cups of coffee, occasionally exchanging it so that we can have a taste of both the drinks. and I find that there is love, so much love stuffed in the atmosphere that I can barely even breathe. and it is then I find the words scratching at my throat, begging to be let out – I love you. I love you. I love you.

and yet, I can never say them to their face. maybe on call, definitely on text, but never to their face. I watch my friends and family share their love freely, openly. They hug each other, say "I love you" without a second thought. And I envy them. I wish I could be like that, to let go of my fears and just be vulnerable. But it's not that simple.

because how can I look them in the eye and tell them that this small four-letter word encompasses all that I feel for them? how can I tell them that this tiny word fosters my relentless gratitude, my undying devotion, and the warmth that I feel coursing through my veins just in their presence. how do I minimize such a monumental feeling in this four-letter word? unfair, isn't it?

four letters aren't enough to show them how deeply this feeling is embedded in my veins, in my atoms, how it is carved into every layer or my skin and every time I close my eyes, I can see this abstract feeling imprinted on the back of my eyelids.

I love you. I love you. I love you.

I love you so much that it makes me angry. I love you so much that it fills me up with this insane amount of guilt. I love you so much that it kills me not being able to lay myself bare in front of you. because, darling, if you could see yourself the way I do, you would understand why I worship you the way Icarus worshipped the sun. I love you so much that despite not being able to keep you from all harm, I would set myself on fire if it meant keeping you warm. I love you so much that I cannot imagine a world where you didn't exist. you're a part of me. in this life and also in the next.

my love is visceral, unfiltered and rugged, and sadly, I never learnt how to be entirely vulnerable. so, yes, I don't know how to tell this to you but if you were to dismantle this piece of my heart and restructure it, it'd take the shape of your face. so, of course. I fucking love you. even if I don't say it. even if I will never say it.

I love you. I love you. I love you.

ECLIPSE

They're polar opposites, they hardly ever coexist!

It's a tradition! Since the dawn of time, it persists.

There's no debating the fact that they're meant to be,

Yet every single day, it's only a glimpse of each other they could see.

In the summers, since times immemorial, the warm zephyr blew,

The birds, bees and the flowers, danced on their toes.

The sun's splendour magnified out by the sea,

Bringing with it a sense of calm and serenity.

All day long, the sun in all its glory burned bright

But it paved way for its lover, the moment night started to rise.

The night strode into the sky, holding Moon's hand,

And that is where this epic love story once began.

The planets came to watch, the stars gathered round,

The birds went quiet, ceasing their euphonious sound.

The lovers meet for a while, a feather light touch of their hands,

Just staring at each other until the one of them decides to land.

Sun and Moon are but two lovers who rarely ever meet,

They always chase each other, forever incomplete.

They always miss each other by a fraction of a second,

Waiting for the new day to rise, to make their amends.

Spring is their favourite season of the year,

It's the time in their eternity that they hold extremely dear.

Because while the fragrant winds of the spring blows,

They get to stare at each other's eyes, at least for an hour or so.

But, once in a while, they do tend to meet,

Once in a while they get to feel complete.

They get to touch each other and enjoy their overdue kiss,

As the entire world basks in the splendour of their eclipse.

21

NOT YOUR FIRST LOVE

I am not your first love.

Mine are not the first lips that you kissed,

or the first girl that you said you missed.

I am not your first.

I am not the first person to hold your hand in the hallway

or the first one you let walk through your heart's doorway

because she was there before me.

she was there in every core memory,

her voice as sweet as that of a canary,

so, tell me, how am I supposed to compete with someone of her majesty.

I can't.

because her essence is ingrained in the walls of your heart's arteries,

floating through the blood that courses through your veins.

and I can't go through the pain of not being enough, all over again.

so yes, I can't compete because I am not her

and I can never be her.

but, I am a girl that dipped her hands in blood

for a boy who taught me it's exactly what you do when you're in love.

everything that hurts so bad always starts with a subtle ache.

you never know you're so deeply in love until you line up all your stakes.

so, when you tell me now that you love me
and I tell you that I love you too,
do you still reminisce the way she used to love you?
every time my hand grazes yours,
every word that falls through your mouth,
every kiss that touches my skin,
does she still linger beneath every sentence that passes through your lips?

why are you so quiet; what is going on in your head,
at least respect me enough to give me an answer, is what I've always said.
should I just back the fuck off or keep trying
to ignite that flame of passion that keeps simmering as I keep crying
because every second I spend with you makes me feel like I'm dying.
sweetheart, I need you to give me something to hold on to,
please, tell me what can I do to see this, us, through?

your silence is an answer in itself, and I won't push you to talk
if that isn't what you want
but just tell me one thing – one thing before I burst,
before my remaining composure turns to dust,

today, when you told me that you love me
were you really thinking about how you loved her first?

22

APOLOGIZING

I think I will never be able to stop apologizing
woven words like silk, their weight feels paralyzing,
like an endless echo, my lament, forever agonizing.

lurking in the shadows deep, my soul hides from the light
a sorry spectre, lost in the ministrations of the night.
with a chalice of remorse, I am daily baptized
apologies slipping through my lips, as if they could stop the ship's capsize.
I bare my soul, my deepest scars unfurled,
but each word I utter binds me further to the world.
a world that gave me nothing but heartache and dysphoria
while I scrounged through the rags for even the tiniest amount of euphoria.
with each breath, my heart abides, the venomous words fed to me yell 'surprise!'
the people I would've once gone to war for, I now despise
I hate myself for this sudden flip, so I bow down and apologize.

for the bubbling anger I can't keep in check
for the words I said when I was an emotional wreck.
for the conversations where I laid myself begrudgingly bare,
for the times I said, *"I need a friend, can you please come down here?"*
for shrinking away when I needed a touch,

for fearing you'd see me as a nuisance, see me as 'too much'.

for not trusting you'd catch me if I fell apart,

for masochistically tearing down my own fucking heart.

for the wars I lost that I promise you I'd win,

for the scars that slipped through gracing the surface of my skin.

I apologize to those who glimpse my twisted mind,

or the storm within, where sanity's confined,

I am ensnared by this never-ending wave of remorse and dread

if only I could travel through time and say something but also take back

the words I said.

a wraith of guilt, I drift alone, writhing in psychosomatic pain

while all my unvoiced apologies like poison slither through my veins.

the weight of sins, like heavy stones weigh me down

lament, distrust and disgrace make up my iron crown.

oh, you can take a breath and quit the chastising,

you've conditioned me enough that I will never - *never* - be able to stop

apologizing.

23

MAYBE

maybe if I were prettier, sharper, crafted from something more divine,
you wouldn't flinch at the thought of me, as if my presence was a curse by design.
as if I bled into your life just to unravel its seams,
as if I syphoned away your peace, leaving only the wreckage of your dreams.
maybe if I was still and firm, like a glass that never breaks,
you'd finally see me as worth your time, not just a string of your mistakes.

maybe if I were subtler, my presence a fleeting sensation,
you'd still glance my way and without hesitation.
as if I wasn't the person to blame for everything wrong in your life,
as if my mere existence in the same plane as yours wasn't really a crime.
maybe if I was less, just a shadow in your mind,
you wouldn't look at me as something you needed to leave behind.

maybe if I were quieter, soft as the whispering wind through trees,
you would think twice before leaving me bleeding, begging, down on my knees!
as if my words didn't matter, they could simply fade,
as if I could leave them in my mind's shadow until they completely desecrate!

maybe if I was hollow, empty enough to let you breathe,

you wouldn't see me as the chains you wear, a reason you must leave.

maybe if I wasn't a writer, spilling ink instead of tears,

you'd see me beyond the sadness, beyond the confines of my fears.

as if I could live without turning everything into art,

as if my pen wasn't the only way I know how to speak my heart.

maybe if I wasn't always searching for meaning in the pain,

you'd still find me real, not just a ghost trying desperately to remain.

maybe if I could silence the constant questioning in my head,

I wouldn't wonder if I'm the reason you're unhappy and wish me dead.

as if my existence is a burden you carry since I can't make myself lighter

as if after everything, you'd still gather me in your arms and hold tighter.

maybe if I wasn't always searching for what's wrong with me,

I wouldn't feel like a problem waiting to be solved, you see?

maybe if I was less afraid of being left behind,

I wouldn't hold so tightly, wouldn't lose my mind.

as if I could let go without the fear of isolation dangling over my head like

a sword,

as if keeping you near was nothing short of an award.

maybe if I was braver, I'd be the one to disappear,

instead of waiting for the day you, my love, will no longer be here.

maybe if I didn't need you to see me, I could stop haunting the spaces between us,

and quit trying to make myself smaller, a shadow in the fuss.

as if I could fade into silence, a ghost with a heart that's sore,

as if just by being less, I could find a way to be loved more.

maybe if I vanished completely, you'd finally feel the loss,

but I'm trapped in this longing, a heart that pays the cost.

maybe if I could still bleed and wasn't merely a well of sorrow,

you could feel my heart still ache, thinking "maybe it'll be better tomorrow!"

as if I were still human, albeit just a fraction,

not just a vessel of empathy, a relentless fountain of unending compassion.

after all, maybe if I weren't so lost in the shadows of your gaze,

I'd find the strength to leave and not just waste away in your haze.

PART 5

ALL I EVER DID

at the end of the day, it's all about what we felt and what we did,

and all I ever did, apparently, was hide and crib.

I built walls, solidifying them into a fortress, brick by brick,

but every wall hid a wound, a scar too thick.

my heart was a garden, but I never loved it enough to water it,

leaving it to rot, every petal I let wilt.

I told myself it was safer this way,

but now I wonder if I've buried pieces of me too far to say.

in the dark of my mind, I built a nest of regret,

a filthy cocoon where my thoughts slowly bled.

I reached out, but my fingers were full of rust,

trying to hold onto things that, in the palms of my hand, turned to dust.

every moment I thought I'd heal in time,

I sliced open my skin and called it a rhyme.

at the end of the day, I stand here in shattered lore -

I didn't live, just locked myself behind closed doors.

BEFORE I THROW IT IN THE TRASH CAN

ages ago, I remember telling myself, 'Shreya, if nothing seems to go right, write." & I kept it like an oath.

but, if there was something I could tell all my writings, I'd say that I'm sorry. because they deserved better than to be the epicentre of my wrath & become the sonnet of my scars. every time I picked up my pen, I pricked a poor paper with thorns & raked my pen through it until it was all sliced & torn. I hung my heart in the balcony of solitude & drowned myself in a pool of crimson with my feelings pushing my head under. who knew writing could be so brutal? yet, as the world stabbed me & as these transiently familiar words watched me bleed ink, writing patched me up.

instead of endorphins, when my body was secreting bile, I stifled it in my throat & looked for a place in the endless darkness to hide. it was like the dark is chasing me & everything is closing in on me. that is when I found it – writing. I was a living soul, grieving a long dead heart & it was words that wrapped me in their arms. I sewed a fabric of oblivious thoughts & my conscious words, spinning it into a carelessly worded prose or excruciatingly visceral poetry. for it was those words that printed my soul on a white piece of paper.

whoever said that white is the color of peace, had it all wrong. It is emptiness – a void created in the absence of all other colors & when my blue ink stained a paper's whiteness, I felt oceans full of emotions spilling from the seams of my shut eyes, from the space between the fingers of my clenched fists & the whimpers falling out of my dried mouth. it was my proses & poems that sat through the myriad funerals of my past selves, each one dying in their embrace & its heir rising from the words carved into their chests. still, I had the audacity to annihilate them.

I'd tell them I am sorry that I never truly let them see the light of the day. now that I think about it, it's probably because I am too afraid of my true self & my writings, are as real as I get. when I look in the mirror, I'm afraid of what I'll see so I throw it all away. Nevertheless, I know they still exist. somewhere at the edge of the void, buried within layers & layers of my flawless skin. they still live in the silence between my thoughts & are the heinous & beastly part of me that I keep hidden from the rest of the world.

every time I read what I've written in my inadvertent fit of paranoia & anxiety, I can see the words rearrange themselves & read out the exact same thing every single fucking time –

'are you okay? are we okay? are we ever going to be okay?'

before I throw them in the trash can.

26

I WAS ONCE A WRITER

Once upon a time, I was a writer, and the world was my oyster. But today, I am a broken shell of a woman I once used to be, tattered, and shattered; broken and despaired; but still wandering the endless corridors with my diary and pen tucked close to my chest.

My mind is aggressively begging me to create something potent. It's coercing me into writing something because it's been sixty-six days today and I still haven't picked up the pen to even strike a line on paper. My prime source of contentment and self-satisfaction is based on my capability to create a series of writings that I can sign off as my own but recently, nothing fits the bill. I do not know what or whom to write about because my muse is dormant. Still, I force myself to pick up the pen and take a trip down the memory lane because if my present isn't letting me write, maybe something in my past will trigger something. That is when I come across your face. Again.

Even in my memory, your face is still as crisp as the fresh page of a notebook on the first day of school. Two months without seeing you or having any contact with you may as well have been two decades. So, as the pitiful writer that I am, I resort to writing about you – a person whose memories don't even bring a wave of pleasantness anymore. I want to write about you, but I also do not want you to know or understand that what I'm conjuring is about describing you. I know I am taking a risk verbalizing my thoughts and putting my feelings into words for there is a chance that you might come across them and find traces of yourself littered in these words. For that would make me sound like a desperate damsel, waiting for my knight in shining armour to ride through the town with his cavalry. Even if it's to stab me in the heart.

Either way, since you're not supposed to be let into the secret that you were my muse, I shouldn't write about you in the first place, correct? Regardless, the moment I pick up my pen, the first word that I scribble, after being on a twenty-one days' hiatus, is your name in cursive – elegant, radiant, and regal, everything that I thought you were. Before you decided to shed your mask and stopped pretending that you were the very descendent of eros, and I, your Aphrodite. I couldn't bear that the person who made my heart go wild and soar in the open skies has now forced me to bubble wrap it. After all, if you were to stab me still, at least the bubble wrap would cushion the force.

It must be a fantastic feeling knowing that even after ridding myself of you, I can't rid my mind of your thoughts, the feel of your eyes on me, and the touch of your fingers on my back. You would be elated knowing that you are a topic I can't let go of. The writer in me is detrimentally fond of you and is hungry to explore all the emotions you instill in her. Presently, you are the source of my abject mortification but for the writer in me, you're a shining subject to weave my writings around. She is relentlessly clinging on to the feelings you awoke in her because if nothing else, it will give her something to feel – ravenous rage at your vicious vanity, debilitating despair at your impudent infidelity, and of course, bashful betrayal at your open objectification of my feelings. After all, feeling something is better than feeling nothing at all, right?

So, no matter how bad you did me, baby, no matter how long you dragged my carcass across the streets of our town, my mind still finds its way back to you. I know I will probably never see you again and that knowledge is enough to make my heart ache. It makes me feel angry at myself because despite being absolutely shredded at your hands, I still can't stop myself from yearning for those exact same hands. Calloused and stained with blood.

I know you probably won't ever think about me again and that's okay. Because I would do enough thinking for both of us. I will keep you tucked in the pages of my favorite diary, in the smell of moonflowers that you excitedly planted in our garden and between the curves of every single word I would ever write.

I will write my words despite knowing that you're not the best person to write about – after all, you didn't want the world knowing our story, right?

But I think it's because I am so used to writing about you that I never learned how *not* to write about you.

27

LATELY

lately, I have been feeling distant from everyone I have ever known

tell me, God, is this what it feels like to be grown?

unanswered calls, seen-zoned texts,

cancelled plans, lit cigarettes.

a devil-worshiper, a cultist, an epitome of malevolence.

my solitude, a religion I practice with utmost diligence.

my life is on a standstill, I can't seem to move forward,

stuck in the same old shitty town; a cheap, run-down, fucking coward!

I can't face my friends and family; my kith and kin,

buried under the backbreaking weight of my own incorrigible sins.

"I am proud of you, Shreya." is all I yearn to hear,

but apparently, the cross of my existence is just too much to bear.

I am losing faith, but nobody can tell,

so, I might as well sign up for permanent residency in hell.

deep breaths, my love, in and out,

you're too far gone; they won't hear you shout.

"you smoke because you just don't want to talk!"

gee, would you like a medal for stating the obvious, Sherlock?

shutting people out, I locked myself in,

a stream of I am sorrys tumbling from my lips.

I am sorry, I forgot how to text you back,

I forgot how to keep my life on track.

I can't keep my work aside while talking to you on call,

I can't seem to cushion your tumble every time you fall.

I am sorry for texting you when I was a mess,

when I voiced my thoughts, my fears I addressed.

I am sorry I cancel plans every weekend,

I think I am going off the deep end.

I loathe the broken, selfish friendships that seem to follow me around

like a wraith hanging off my neck, the regret, my shroud.

"why, why, why!' it's always a question when I try to confide,

"I don't know, bro!" yes, I do. I fucking lied.

almost a decade down the lane and I still get queasy,

every time something happens, my faith in you goes woozy.

who could've walked away from me, who could've stayed?

yes, you did, but, honey, what was the price you paid?

I wish I learned how to talk even when I am at my worst

to control the break in my voice when I iterate my thoughts, unrehearsed.

if I don't text or call, would we ever talk?

well, rest assured, your profile I will still always stalk.

if you text me today, I might not revert, I might leave you on read,

because I'm trapped inside my head, where all my words are dead.

I can't bridge the gap between who I was and who I've become,

a shattered version of myself, barely holding on.

the lies, the distance, the things I never said,

they pile up like bricks, heavy and dead.

I keep thinking, *maybe tomorrow*, maybe then I'll break free,

but tomorrow never comes, and I'm still here—unseen, unheard, just *me*.

maybe you'll wait, maybe you'll walk away,

I wouldn't blame you, because honestly, I'm so far gone, I don't

know how to stay.

a ghost in my own life, I fade with every call,

I'm sorry, my love, because lately, I can't seem to be anything at all.

28

BLOOD MOON

I peeked out my window and saw the blushing moon in an intriguing conversation with the sky, taking in updates about the sun, the stars and everything that the sky encompasses.

it got me thinking that every time we humans are upset, we tend to scream, wail, and yell our prayers out to the sky. what if the reason why we find solace in the moon is because the sky confides in that gigantic ball of gas, all of our miseries? what if the craters on the moon are a result of the wails of agony that the sky keeps flinging at her – the battle scars that the moon shares with some of us. what if that's the reason why we feel so comfortable in the presence of the moon. because unlike the humans walking the face of this earth saying – 'oh, I know how you feel', and lie, moon, for that matter, really does know what it feels like. It burns with us, it writhes with us, it changes its phases with us. sometimes it's whole and sometimes it's a modicum of what it's capable of and sometimes, it's absent altogether. but there is safety in the knowledge that it'll come back again.

today, the moon is a bright red – the blood moon as it is christened – the color of my love and the blood that poured out of every nick that you left on me over the years.

it took me a terribly long time to understand that you can love someone deeply, but you can't always save them. as much as you'd like to believe that love is the ultimate cure, the one-size-fits-all for every broken person in the world; it isn't.

love, as pure and visceral as it might be, can't fix everything. It can't fix everyone. but then again, the color of love and the color of fresh blood is the same. so, if love can't fix it, then maybe, blood can.

after all, it always ends in blood, doesn't it? It's just the matter of whose.

PART 6

29

MAYBE IN ANOTHER UNIVERSE

maybe in another universe, I gave a fuck when my friend told me that she broke off her three-year relationship with the love of her life. I didn't stand there like a mime, my brown eyes empty as her black ones brimmed with unshed tears - three years, gone, the love of her life, gone. maybe, I pulled her into my arms, held her as her body convulsed with sobs, whispered words that could at least some sense of comfort, albeit temporary. but here? here, I let her fall. I let her hit the ground with no arms to catch her, no voice to soften the blow of the betrayal she felt, and no friend for her bruised and battered heart to lean on. all I felt here was the emptiness of my own indifference, a hollow nothingness where compassion should have been swimming.

maybe in another universe, I would've felt a pang of worry when his message came through - *I'm quite unwell* - and not the cold, dismissive thought that this was just another excuse to dodge my calls. maybe in that universe, I would've called back immediately, my voice soft with concern, ready to meet him where he was, no matter how far. but here, I stared at the screen, the words blurring and my mind racing, wondering if this was just a ruse, if his claim was real, and if I even cared enough to find out. I didn't. I put the phone down, the silence between us louder than any truth I could bear to face.

maybe in another universe, I didn't shut down and sit alone on the worst days of my life, cradling my silence like a lifeline, pretending it didn't choke me. maybe there, I knew how to unlock the doors I kept bolted, especially when someone knocked. I learned how to let people in without the paralyzing fear that they'd see the mess inside and leave. maybe I learned how to speak my heart and be true to my own self and her needs, to trust that the wreckage inside wouldn't scare them away, to believe that I was worth staying for. but here, I am an island, just one tsunami away from disappearing from existence.

maybe in another universe, I didn't bury my feelings beneath punchlines, didn't turn them into jokes sharp enough to keep everyone at an arm's length. maybe there, I learned how to let my guard down, how to let people in, how to say, *I'm hurt*, or *I'm scared*, without disguising it in laughter that echoed too loud in the vacuum of my abandonment. but here, I let every emotion slip through my fingers, flung them into oblivion until they were so far away, I couldn't reach them anymore - until no one ever could.

maybe in another universe, I didn't watch myself self-destruct with a morbid clinical fascination - dissecting my own ruin like it belonged to an outsider. I didn't stare into the mirror, into those empty, lifeless eyes, and turn away like the hollow shell staring back was beyond saving. maybe there I felt something - *anything* - apart from this stifling apathy that suffocated to death the memory of what it felt like to care. but here? here, I let myself stand stoic and calm, detached like a mortician looking over a corpse in the morgue, unable to summon even a breath of grief or guilt for the person I've let disappear (or killed).

maybe in another universe, I wasn't the ghost haunting my own life. I wasn't the villain in my story, always turning away before anyone else could. maybe, I didn't look for reasons to abandon the ones I love before they abandoned me. maybe there, I didn't tear down the bridges I so desperately needed, and I didn't anticipate my grief before it even spawned into existence. maybe in another universe, I wasn't the first to abandon, the first to break. maybe, in that universe, I let myself be loved before I shattered.

maybe in another universe, I didn't crave the pain, the destruction, the agony of forgetting who I was. maybe in another universe, I am not trapped in this prison of my own making. I drift through a city alive with possibility, the pulse of life thrumming in my veins, each heartbeat a reminder that I am here, that I matter. but in this universe, I wake to the suffocating silence of my room, a cocoon of shadows that clings to me like damp fabric, heavy and unyielding.

maybe in another universe, I learned that love wasn't something to fear, but something I was worthy of.

and maybe, just maybe, I allowed myself to stay.

30

BUTTERFLY

hush, little butterfly, rein it all in,

blow your sorrows in puffs of methamphetamine

stifle your heart wrenching shouts.

but breathe, little butterfly in from your nose, out from your mouth,

in and out; inhale and exhale.

fill your lungs with cyanide, with every forthcoming intake

breathe, butterfly, breathe - breathe the air,

adulterated with resentment in the void of care

bask in the back-breaking weight of exacerbate expectations,

of venomous vacations, saddened stations, discombobulated directions,

mangled manifestations

but never - ever - raise your voice against my discretions.

I say you're afraid, you shiver in fright,

I tell you the sky is falling down - you consider that it might,

I tell you, you messed up - you think about it until you can't stand upright

and when I play the ploy that you can breathe -

you breathe, little butterfly,

you breathe until the water fills in your lungs,

until your fingers are pruned, you circle back to the intrusive thought that

your future is doomed,

and your will to survive is consumed.

because maybe you deserve to breathe the misty remains of every broken
shard of dream you ever held in your hands,
to smile and say "it's all alright" until shit hits the fan!
but no, little butterfly - BREATHE.

just. fucking. breathe.

31

TIRED

The days before my birthday have always felt like a quiet unravelling. Everything within me seems to split open, threads of who I am tugged loose by invisible hands. I am a vessel in limbo, a body stretched across the thin membrane of time. Today, I house two tenants: a 21-year-old ghost and a 22-year-old shadow. One fading, the other forming.

The ghost lingers, reluctant to leave. She is the greatest thing you'll ever lose, Shreya - a mosaic of triumphs and trials, mistakes and miracles. She walks through me with weary pride, whispering stories of resilience into my bones. She doesn't say it out loud, but I feel it in the way our shoulders slump at the end of the day, in the way she touches your face when no one's looking. She is tired, Shreya. Tired in a way that only those who have fought their battles alone can be. And yet, she's so much stronger than either of us ever realized. She carried you here, through storms that left scars on your skin and chaos that settled in your mind. She made it.

The shadow looms, impatient yet uncertain, pressing against the walls of my skin. She smells of change - of risks, possibilities, and quiet revolutions. She is hungry, ready to claim her time, to thread new paths through the chaos you call life. She holds no nostalgia, only an unrelenting drive. But she does not yet know the weight of carrying us forward. She will learn.

And I am torn in this tug of war between them. My muscles ache from the dual existence, my heart beats two rhythms - one a eulogy, the other an anthem.

Dear 21-year-old Shreya, I see it now - I see your weariness. You've been holding us together with sheer grit, with that quiet, relentless defiance. You're tired, aren't you? It's okay. I need you to know I am proud of you. Your part in this story is written, and it is glorious. I will hold you until it's time for you to finally let you go.

Shreya, I know how much it hurts to let go. I've held the ache of it in your chest, the heaviness of it in your spine. Your 21-year-old self was extraordinary in her imperfections, her strength, her sheer will to keep moving forward when everything tried to pull her down. But she is not meant to stay. Sweetheart, you must say goodbye. Not gently, for she deserves better than platitudes and soft farewells. Grieve her loss with all the darkness she endured. Honor her strength with every sob. Let her know she mattered.

And then, let the shadow take the reins. She is not here to replace but to inherit, to build upon the ashes of what your 21-year-old self forged. You will grow with her, stretch into spaces you once feared. You will falter, yes, but you will also thrive. Your 22-year-old self is waiting for you to trust her, to step into her skin and let her show you the things she can do. She wants to hold you differently, to carry you with more grace, more purpose, more hope.

But tonight, in this liminal space, I hold them both. I cradle the one who's leaving and the one who's arriving. I am your body, Shreya, and I will bear this transition with all the tenderness you cannot yet give yourself. As we sit in the in-between, we house a comatose almost-corpse and a promise, a funeral and a birth. And when the clock strikes midnight on November 29, when the world tilts just slightly to usher in the new, I will let you go, my 21-year-old.

Not because I want to, but because it is time.

And you, my 22-year-old - be ready. The world will not wait. And I will carry you forward, as I always have.

RAGE FEELS LIKE COMING HOME

rage feels like coming home. like crawling back into a bed of broken glass, the sharp shards slicing into my skin, but it's the only thing that makes me feel *alive*.

it's not just anger, it's this gnawing emptiness inside me that needs to be filled, and the only thing that fits is the violence of it all. I don't know when it started—maybe it was always there, waiting for me to stop pretending I could outrun it. I welcome it, let it claw through my veins like fire, burning away the parts of me that used to care, used to hope.

it feels *right* - like everything else has been a lie, and this raw, ugly feeling is the only truth I can hold on to. I can't tell where the rage ends and I begin anymore. I just know it's the only thing that makes me feel anything at all.

and that thought - *that* thought - is what scares me the most.

IT ISN'T THAT HARD TO BE KIND

it really isn't that hard to be kind, you know?

in the world where compassion hides,

being a young adult is a treacherous fucking ride.

here, judgment's the currency, it's traded and sold,

kindness discarded, as hearts turn cold.

hushed whispers penetrating the air,

adulterating the atmosphere in the void of care.

'Who am I? what am I even doing here?' questions arise left and right

but it isn't enough because we'd rather add on to each other's plight.

in the chaos of identity's uncertain panorama,

please allow me to introduce the term "Intragenerational Trauma" -

a silent, haunting, devastating, enigma.

'If I'm suffering, so should you,' the unwritten creed,

binding us in shared pain, it's become a collective need.

when venomous words fly, and shame's the decree,

women pitted against women, what the fuck is happening to society?

slut-shamed and crucified it all started as a seemingly harmless prank,

but ended in the gallows of the poison that we all reluctantly drank.

blind hatred is the generational anthem; everyone marches to its beat

being unnecessarily mean to a random stranger? such a remarkable feat!

"you're savage, girl; omg, you ate! it's just sarcasm, that's how I talk."

well, maybe you should revaluate your mannerisms? just a thought.

basking in the backbreaking weight of societal expectations,

we're buried neck-deep in the sea of our own frustrations.

while the discombobulated manifestations of a distressed damsel

has her reaching into her pitiful arsenal.

"there's still some good in the world that's worth fighting for, after all!"

bullshit is what that's called.

today, I've watched the world fall from my eyes,

and I don't think it will ever – *ever* – be able to rerise.

34

SOMEONE SHOULD HAVE TOLD ME

someone should have told me in life, there's always a price to pay,

for wanting to drop everything and run or even wanting to stay.

that nothing could prepare me for the bends life will bring,

for the nights I'd be screaming into the void; no one hearing me hollering.

or for the nights I'd have to pick myself up piece by piece,

or for the nights I'd be down on my knees, begging for a release.

someone should have told me that my every choice will be carved into me,

and freedom comes with responsibilities, a cage, with no lock, but a key.

what I choose will shape my life and affect my existence,

that Karma will catch up even if I try to hide and avoid the consequences.

that my mind will be the most potent part of my arsenal, but also the most volatile,

that my stoicism wouldn't make me invincible, but vulnerable and vile.

someone should have told me that time doesn't wait, it doesn't bend

it crashes through life, never healing, never making any amends.

that it's a myth, 'you have all the time in the world,'

when the speed of the passing time will actually leave you disturbed.

that every broken piece of me will find a space to occupy - just so it can
stay,

and every dawn will harbour more cracks than I thought I could handle up
until yesterday.

someone should have told me that the loudest silence is in my chest,

the one creeping in with "you're just not enough", though I did my best.

that my love can make empires tumble and fall,

but I can't love someone into loving me no matter what.

that I'd grow up to be a person who freezes at the slightest hint of affection,

or a person who'd be awfully skilled at the art of deflection.

someone should have told me that scars don't fade, they grow

that my demons won't ever vanish, they'll learn how to glow.

the pain I'll bury deep inside would transform into a shadow I can't outrun, that the things I do in a fit of rage, can't always be undone.

the people I once would've gone to war for, are now mere ghosts,

leaving behind empty echoes of their faithless boasts.

someone should have told me that at times there's no help coming from above,

that try as I may, I can't hate myself into a version of me I'd love.

that the mirror will forever reflect the pain I refused to name,

and I will always be the soulless carrier of fountains of blame.

that forgiveness isn't followed by relief; it's a curse, a death so slow,

a quiet surrender where you grieve what you'll probably never let go.

someone should have told me that the things I suppress will never truly stay buried,

they'd lurk in the shadows, waiting to rise like an army of the undead.

that I'll have to question how much I can get away with until it's too much,

until the changes feel like a murder; a quiet killing of who I once was.

that I would think about them more often than I'd care to admit,

some with a fond longing, others while downing in the waves of regret.

someone should have told me that I would lose myself - over and over again,

until the person I once was, is a stranger to me - my 'healing era' in vain.

that healing isn't a gift, it's a constant state of war,

a relentless battle with a self that you're not sure you can restore.

that the scars won't fade, the world wouldn't slow

and one day, in the mirror, I'll meet the monster I never wanted to know.

35

YOU NEED TO FORGIVE YOURSELF

"You need to forgive yourself!" the words echoed in the hollow chambers of my soul, resonating like a distant plea for mercy.

but how? how can I forgive myself for everything that I did to myself?

within the twisted labyrinth of my psyche, a malevolent presence resides, a monstrous spectre forged from the shards of my shattered self-esteem. I look in the mirror and see the tattered remnants of a grotesque self-portrait, something I will never publicly admit to being me. its whispers, like venomous serpents, coil around my consciousness, injecting a paralyzing venom that corrodes my very being. so, tell me, how can I forgive myself for falling so far from grace that I can't even remember the person I used to be.

but what I am is a master of self-sabotage. each misstep, each self-inflicted wound, each selfish indulgence of mine manifests as nightmarish phantoms haunting my existence. they are carefully curated murals on the walls of my conscience narrating a story of despair and decay. they dance in the moonlight of my misery, cacophonous marionettes animated by my own inner tormentor – the little voice in my head telling me that I was never enough and I will never be enough. so, tell me, darling, how do I even begin to forgive myself for being so cruel to my own fucking self.

they told me that making a new life will cost me an old one but they never told me that my old one will still have an iota of a heartbeat, the pulse barely beating, but there nonetheless. the promises I made to myself lay tattered, like the wings of a fallen angel. each vow broken, each dream left to wither, the ashes of my aspirations now scattered in the howling winds of regret. the abhorrent betrayal of my own potential weighs heavily, like a millstone dragging me to the abyss. so, tell me, my love, how do I forgive myself for giving up on myself when I needed it the most?

my reflection in a shattered mirror reveals the carnival of my sins, a hall of mirrors distorting every ounce of self-worth, my self-confidence. my eyes, once pools of hope, now mirror twin pools of despair, and my once-tender skin bears the scarlet tapestry of a thousand self-inflicted wounds, each etched with the cruel blade of my own self-hatred. I hate what I see but I detrimentally love what I am. but the clashes of emotions are too much for my mind to bear, and I run away. like usual. so, tell me, love, how do I forgive myself for abandoning my own reflection?

there's a little girl in my head, curled up, chained to the side of my bedpost with nothing but self-consciousness to keep her company. her eyes, once filled with innocence, now mirror the abyss of my own bafflement. the sturdy chains that bind her are forged from the mistakes I've made, each link a reminder of my reckless choices shaping me into who I am today. every time I close my eyes and dare myself to open the iron gated channels barring her from my vision, I watch her. paralyzed, as she shivers in the darkness, a reflection of every decision that led her... led us, to this desolate place. in the echo chamber of my mind, her silent sobs resonate, merging seamlessly with the haunting chorus of my regrets. how I console her when every attempt at solace is tainted by the knowledge that I am the architect of her confinement, the puppeteer pulling the strings of her misery, the captor and captive, dancing this macabre dance? so, tell me, how do I forgive myself for sculpting her prison from the debris of my own shortcomings?

in the relentless pursuit of salvaging others, I have wrung myself dry, pouring out love and care like an inexhaustible wellspring. for them, I became the person I so desperately needed for myself – a pillar of strength, a bottomless well of compassion. yet, in this ceaseless outpour of care and affection, I failed to replenish the reservoir of self-love within. I navigated the labyrinth of their insecurities, offering solace and understanding, but I neglected the little girl within, chained to the side of my bed, longing for the same tenderness I bestowed upon others. the irony, a bitter pill to swallow, is that I've shown more kindness to strangers than to the one familiar person who bears my name. so, tell me, how can I even begin to forgive myself for being so self-critical that I never learned how to be soft to myself.

and yet, I have the audacity to wonder if I can still seek redemption. if I can still become the person I can blindly trust when I have done nothing but betrayed my own self time and again. now, as I traverse this nightmarish landscape of my own creation, it becomes increasingly apparent that forgiveness is but an apparition, a tantalizing mirage on the barren horizon of my existence. redemption, the illusion of salvation, is a fleeting dream, forever just out of reach. so, tell me now, how do I forgive myself for nourishing my debilitating sanity with specks of hope, until I could hallucinate a fragile ray of light in the suffocating darkness of my own mind?

and so, I remain lost in this circus of self-loathing, the ringmistress of my own doom. the question of how to forgive oneself is a riddle too complex for my fractured mind to solve. in the darkness of my own creation, I am condemned to writhe and suffer, a tortured soul trapped in the prison of my own making, as the shadows of my past grow ever deeper and more suffocating. in this crescendo of self-inflicted despair, the chilling truth lingers: redemption, like a wisp of smoke, slips through the cracks of my splintered consciousness. the finale approaches, and I am left to wander the abyss, forever haunted by the realization that maybe, just maybe, I will never be able to forgive myself.

because, how, how does one forgive the architect of their own damnation?

ACKNOWLEDGEMENTS

Dear Reader,

Well, here we are, at the end of this wonderfully weird journey. You've stuck around through the chaos, the rawness, and the dark corners of my brain—and I have no idea what kind of mental endurance that took, but I appreciate you for it. I hope you felt every ounce of it, even if it made you squirm a little (or a lot). Thank you for hanging in there!

First off, to my father, **Dr. Avnish Vijay**—thank you for being the calm in my storm, even when I was having a full-on emotional hurricane. You probably didn't fully understand what the hell I was doing with these words, but you were always there, steady and patient, even when I was writing in the middle of a meltdown. You might not get it, but you *are* the reason I didn't disappear into the madness.

Mom, **Mrs. Sheetal Vijay,** what can I say? You've been my unshakable cheerleader through every meltdown, every 'I can't do this' moment. If it wasn't for your gentle pushing (and occasionally dragging) me to write, none of this would exist. So, you can have all the credit for this book... and all the blame for making me do this *deep dive* into my soul. You're a legend.

Aryan, my baby brother - thank you for letting me rot away in the confines of my room and bringing me food and making we watch anime every time I sobbed so I forget about everything and type out my weird thoughts. Sure, I know you're secretly cringing at reading this, but I'll take the love while it lasts. You're the best at sharing, even when I'm clearly stealing all your space.

Aman Gupta, my chosen brother, my partner in crime - thank you for being the mastermind behind my most absurd ideas and somehow believing in them. You've watched me fall apart, been the only one who could handle my freak-outs, and yet you've never once told me to shut up (well, not *that* often). I don't know how you do it, but I'm thankful for your constant insanity and support. You're the unsung hero in all of this.

Anjana, love, let's face it, you've been my therapist, sanity check, and emotional punching bag. You've been there for every high, low, and in-between, and somehow always knew when to tell me I was being ridiculous (or when to let me be ridiculous). Without you, these words would've stayed locked in my brain, and we both know that's a tragedy.

Shivi, babe, you've been my personal cheerleader, reality check, and the loudest voice of reason (literally). You always say, "Shreya, if you don't start speaking this very moment..." and honestly, without you, I probably wouldn't have. Your unwavering belief in me, your endless patience, and your ability to call me out when I most needed it have been everything. Thank you, my love.

And to **my friends from university – Raghu, Tapas, Tanishka, Ria, Aditi** (and all of the others) thank you for always being there to listen to my most ridiculous ideas, and for never, ever letting me get away with being "too much." You've managed to survive my nonsensical rants and helped me see the world through a weirder, more chaotic lens. Thank you so much for always pushing me to use my voice, even when I wasn't sure I had one. And also, no more "You don't open up, Shreya" comments, okay? I'm opening up - just not in the way you're used to. Deal with it, guys.

Lastly, to you, my reader, my fellow wanderer through this strange mental maze - thank you for giving this mess of a book a chance. You could've picked any other book out there, and yet you chose this one. You are *now* a part of my madness. Enjoy the ride.

With endless gratitude and just a *little* bit of insanity,

Shreya

AUTHOR'S BIO

Shreya Vijay is an emerging author, poet, and visionary, aiming to help her readers see the world in a different hue via the medium of her writings. Writing has always been Shreya's solace.

She mostly writes dark, deep, and intense poems and prose, which lures the reader in only to teleport them to a world of fantasy, love & borderline mania, all the while holding a firm grip over the essence of reality. All her writings are sure to ``make the reader question their sanity & challenge their perception.

Apart from that, she is also an all-time music addict & a nyctophile. When she is not writing, she can be found with earphones dangling from her ears, grooving to whatever song is her song of the week.